12 EPIC ARCHAEOLOGICAL ADVENTURES

by Carla Mooney

12 STORY LIBRARY

www.12StoryLibrary.com

12-Story Library is an imprint of Bookstaves.

Photographs ©: Christhilf/iStockphoto, cover, 1; Noel Feans/CC2.0, 4; Keystone Pictures USA/ZUMAPRESS/Alamy Stock Photo, 5; Animalparty/CC4.0, 6; Lee Roger Berger research team/CC4.0, 7; thipjang/Shutterstock.com, 8; thipjang/Shutterstock.com, 9; liorpt/iStockphoto, 10; GuilhermeMesquita/Shutterstock.com, 11; undefined undefined/iStockphoto, 12; Teomancimit/CC3.0, 13; Boyce's Images/Shutterstock.com, 14; William Vaughn Tupper/CC2.0, 15; Anton Belo/Shutterstock.com, 16; Orhan Cam/Shutterstock.com, 17; shootmybusiness/Shutterstock.com, 18; shootmybusiness/Shutterstock.com, 19; dmitry_islentev/Shutterstock.com, 20; OSTILL/iStockphoto, 21; OSTILL/iStockphoto, 22; Sarahshine/CC4.0, 23; RPBMedia/iStockphoto, 24; RPBMedia/iStockphoto, 25; National Photo Company Collection/Library of Congress, 26; Larry Porges/Shutterstock.com, 27; pingebat/Shutterstock.com, 28-29

ISBN
978-1-63235-564-5 (hardcover)
978-1-63235-618-5 (paperback)
978-1-63235-680-2 (hosted ebook)

Library of Congress Control Number: 2018937845

About the Cover
Moai figures on Easter Island in Polynesia.

Table of Contents

1 Olduvai Gorge Holds Clues about Early Humans

Olduvai Gorge is part of the Great Rift Valley in Tanzania, Africa. Millions of years ago, volcanoes spread layers of ash and rocks across the area. About 30,000 years ago, draining water began carving through the ash and rock. Erosion slowly formed the gorge. Layers up to two million years old were exposed.

Olduvai Gorge holds many clues about our early human ancestors. Scientists have uncovered hundreds of fossils. In the 1930s, archaeologists Louis and Mary Leakey began large excavations at Olduvai Gorge. They made several important discoveries. They uncovered stone tools

The gorge is also called the Cradle of Mankind.

and fossilized bones of early human species.

One morning, Mary Leakey made one of their most famous discoveries. She found pieces of a skull. They belonged to a new species of early human called *Paranthropus boisei.* The discovery became known as Nutcracker Man. Scientists estimated Nutcracker Man was about 1.75 million years old. Later, the Leakeys found fossil evidence of another early human species called *Homo habilis.* It was dated to be about two million years old. The Leakeys' work sparked interest in the study of human evolution.

Today, archaeologists still work at Olduvai Gorge. Visitors can tour the excavation sites and visit a museum. The museum holds a collection of early human fossils and stone tools.

30

Number of miles (48.2 km) that Olduvai Gorge stretches in length.

- Olduvai Gorge was formed nearly 30,000 years ago.
- Scientists have uncovered hundreds of fossils of early humans and stone tools.
- Louis and Mary Leakey found fossilized bones of *Homo habilis*, an early human that lived about two million years ago.

Mary and Louis Leakey at a dig site.

2

Discovering *Homo naledi* at Rising Star Cave

In 2013, two cavers found some ancient bones in Rising Star Cave. The cave is near Johannesburg, South Africa. When scientists came to excavate the bones, they discovered nearly 1,500 fossil remains. There were bones from at least 15 individuals.

In 2015, scientists announced these bones were from a new species of early human. It was called *Homo naledi*. It had a mix of ancient and modern human features. Its brain was about the size of an orange. Its hands were human-like, but the fingers were locked into a curve. This suggests that *Homo naledi* climbed and used tools. It stood about five feet tall, with long legs and feet almost identical to human feet today. This suggests that *Homo naledi* could walk long distances. Many scientists believe it could be one of our earliest human relatives.

There are still many questions about *Homo naledi*. How old are the bones? How did they get into the cave? How does *Homo naledi* fit into the human family tree? Scientists are working to answer these questions. They hope to learn more about how *Homo naledi* fits into the history of humans.

The Dinaledi Chamber is the innermost room of the cave where the bones were discovered.

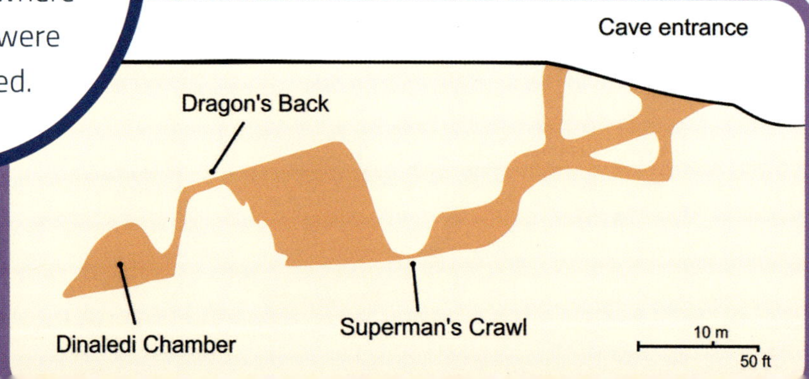

7

Width in inches (17.8 cm) of the gap skinny scientists squeezed through to reach the fossils in Rising Star Cave.

- In Rising Star Cave, scientists have uncovered hundreds of fossils belonging to a new species of early human.
- *Homo naledi's* fossils show a mix of ancient and modern human features.
- Scientists believe that *Homo naledi* might be one of our earliest human relatives.

Scientists believe *Homo naledi* is between 236,000 and 335,000 thousand years old.

3

Lascaux Cave Displays Early Cave Paintings

DISCOVERING THE CAVE

In 1940, four boys followed their dog down a narrow entrance to a cavern. The boys discovered the first artwork on the Lascaux cave walls. The next day, they returned to the cave and explored deeper parts. They told their teacher, who alerted the proper officials. Excavation of the cave began.

Lascaux Cave is located in southwestern France. It is home to some of the world's most famous prehistoric cave paintings. Nearly 600 paintings decorate the walls. The paintings mostly feature animals that lived in the area. There are horses, deer, bison, and even cats. The cave also holds about 1,400 engravings.

Scientists believe the artwork was created by humans who lived around 17,000 to 15,000 BCE. They may

Many paintings are of animals.

Digital photography, 3-D printing, and laser imaging were used to replicate the paintings for Lascaux IV.

have used the cave as a place for religious and hunting rituals.

Most of the paintings on the walls were made with mineral pigments. Mineral pigments are naturally occurring minerals that were used as coloring in early paints. The painters applied the pigments with their fingers or brushes made of hair or moss. They blew pigments through hollow bones.

In 1963, Lascaux Cave was closed to the public. The moisture from human breath had caused mold to form on the paintings. Artificial lighting had faded the pigments. Today, a replica of the Lascaux cave called Lascaux IV receives thousands of visitors each day.

1

Number of humans featured in the Lascaux Cave's paintings and engravings.

- Lascaux Cave holds some of the world's most famous prehistoric cave paintings.
- Scientists believe the paintings were created by humans who lived around 17,000 to 15,000 BCE.
- Most paintings are of animals that lived in the area.

4 Masada Is a Link to Ancient Israel

Masada sits atop an isolated cliff in Israel. The cliff is at the western end of the Judean Desert. It overlooks the Dead Sea. Masada is a site of great natural beauty and archaeological importance. The 840-acre (340-hectare) complex holds well-preserved ruins from the ancient kingdom of Israel.

Masada was built by King Herod the Great, who ruled Judaea between 37 BCE and 4 CE. He built palaces, storerooms, barracks, cisterns, and an armory. He surrounded Masada with a wall. After Herod's death, the Roman Empire took over Judaea. In 66 CE, a group of Jewish rebels took over Masada. After the Romans destroyed Jerusalem in 70 CE, they turned their forces against Masada.

The fortress held fewer than 1,000 rebels. Many were women and children. A Roman army besieged

Masada means "fortress" in Hebrew.

This cavern was an underground water tank for the fortress.

Masada. They blockaded the complex and cut the people off from help. They built camps and an attack ramp. The Romans finally broke through the wall. The Jewish rebels knew they would become Roman slaves. They took their own lives instead.

For more than 13 centuries, no one came to Masada. The desert helped to protect it from visitors or settlers. In 1828, scholars found it. Ever since, archaeologists have been studying the complex. In 1966, Masada and its surroundings were made a National Park.

40,000

Cubic meters of water (10,566,882 gallons) held by Masada's cisterns.

- The Masada site dates back to the ancient kingdom of Israel.
- It was built by Herod the Great, who ruled Judaea between 37 BCE and 4 CE.
- It was the site of the Jewish rebels' last stand against the Roman army.

THINK ABOUT IT

What are some things we can learn from visiting historic sites? Is there a site somewhere in the world you would like to visit someday? What would you hope to learn?

5 Gobekli Tepe's Pillars Remain a Mystery

A hill rises from the ground in southeastern Turkey. At the top is a depression that looks like a belly button. The hill is called Gobekli Tepe, which means Potbelly Hill. It is home to a monumental structure. Tall stone pillars are connected by stone walls in circular patterns. At the center of each group are two pillars surrounded by smaller stones.

Archaeologists have unearthed many megalith structures at Gobekli Tepe. They believe there may be more buried around the site. Some of the standing stones at Gobekli Tepe are blank. Others are carved with foxes, lions, snakes, wild boars, vultures, and other symbols.

Archaeologists believe that Gobekli Tepe was built around 10,000 BCE. Some think it might be the world's first temple. But people who lived that long ago did not know how to farm and grow crops.

The pillars are made of limestone and weigh as much as 50 tons (45 metric t) each.

Scholars were sure that farming came first, before people started building temples. Now they are not so sure. Maybe building Gobekli Tepe brought people together and then they learned to farm.

Around 8,000 BCE, the site was filled in with dirt. The dirt contained many thousands of pieces of animal bones. Some of the bones are from animals now extinct. Scientists don't know why the site was filled in. Almost everything about Gobekli Tepe is still a mystery.

16

Height in feet (5 m) of the tallest pillars discovered at Gobekli Tepe.

- Gobekli Tepe is a large structure made of pillars connected by stone walls that form circles or ovals.
- It was built around 10,000 BCE and buried about 1,000 years later.
- Some archaeologists believe that Gobekli Tepe may be the world's oldest temple.

The animal carvings suggest animal worship or belief in animal-like gods.

6

The Pyramids of Giza Stand the Test of Time

The pyramids were originally covered in polished white limestone.

2.3 million

Number of limestone blocks used to build the Great Pyramid at Giza.

- The Pyramids of Giza were built about 4,500 years ago.
- The pyramids were built as tombs for the Egyptian Pharaohs.
- Artwork and text found inside the pyramids tell us about life in ancient Egypt.

The three Pyramids of Giza have stood for more than 4,500 years. Egypt's kings, called pharaohs, built the pyramids as tombs. They believed that pharaohs became kings of the dead. They filled their pyramids with everything they would need in the afterlife. When a pharaoh died, he was mummified and placed in the pyramid.

The oldest pyramid was built for Pharaoh Khufu. It is also the largest, rising about 481 feet (147 m) from

This scrapbook page, c.1860-1890, details the Great Pyramid's chambers and passageways.

the ground. The middle pyramid is the tomb of Khafre, Khufu's son. The third and smallest pyramid is the tomb of Pharaoh Menkaure.

Scientists are still working to understand how the ancient Egyptians built the pyramids. They know that the builders were skilled Egyptian workers. Some experts believe the workers and building supplies came from communities all across Egypt.

Inside the pyramids, scientists can learn about life in ancient Egypt. Art on the walls shows scenes of how Egyptians lived. Inscriptions and texts reveal clues about the Egyptian language.

THE GREAT SPHINX

Pharaoh Khafre built the Great Sphinx as part of his pyramid complex. Made from limestone, it has a lion's body and a man's head. It is 66 feet high (20 m) and 240 feet long (73 m). The Sphinx is one of the largest monolithic structures in the world. Some archaeologists believe it represents the Pharaoh in the form of the sun god Ra.

7

Ancient Tombs Found in the Valley of the Kings

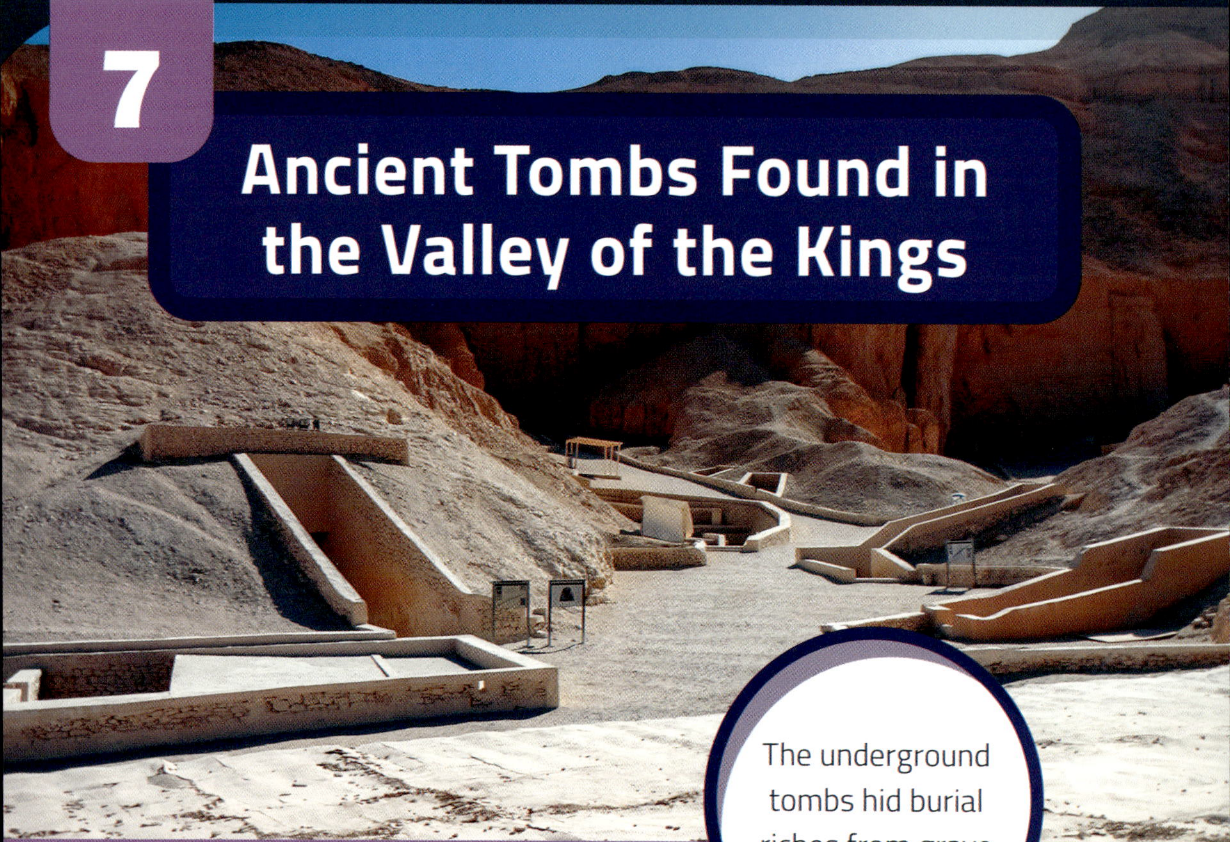

The underground tombs hid burial riches from grave robbers.

Ancient Egyptians took great care with their dead. They preserved their bodies and created underground tombs for them. One of the most famous groups of tombs is in the Valley of the Kings, near the city of Luxor. Pharaohs, queens, and high priests were buried there during the New Kingdom, which lasted from 1539 to 1075 BCE. There are more than 60 tombs in the Valley of the Kings. Some are small. Others are very large, with over 100 underground chambers.

22.5

Weight in pounds (10 kg) of King Tut's death mask.

- The Valley of the Kings was a burial ground for pharaohs, queens, and high priests.
- More than 60 tombs have been found there.
- King Tut's tomb was discovered in 1922.

The most famous tomb in the Valley of the Kings belongs to Pharaoh Tutankhamun, also known as King Tut. He ruled Egypt from about age nine until he was nineteen. He died around 1324 BCE. King Tut's tomb was discovered in 1922. It held many treasures including the King's mummy, jewelry, and statues. They revealed much about royal life in ancient Egypt.

Today, archaeologists are still working in the Valley of Kings. They want to learn more about ancient Egypt. They believe that many tombs are waiting under the sand to be discovered.

KING TUT'S CURSE

Since King Tut's tomb was discovered, rumors have swirled about it. One says that anyone who disturbs the tomb will face a terrible curse. The legend grew stronger after a few people involved in the tomb's discovery died. Some people claim the curse was invented by Howard Carter, who led the excavation team. He wanted to keep intruders away from his history-making discovery.

Tutankhamen's Mask is the main attraction in the Egyptian Museum in Cairo.

8

A Thousand Years to Build Stonehenge

Near Salisbury, England, Stonehenge is a large circle of standing stones. Built thousands of years ago, it is one of the world's most famous prehistoric monuments. It is also one of the world's biggest mysteries.

Archaeologists believe that work on Stonehenge began about 5,000 years ago. It was built in several stages over more than 1,000 years. Building Stonehenge took a huge effort from many people. Generations built and rebuilt Stonehenge, changing it each time.

CLUES IN THE HEEL STONE

In the northern hemisphere, June 21 is the longest day of the year. Every June 21 at Stonehenge, the sun rises over the Heel Stone. December 21 is the shortest day of the year. That's when the sun sets over the Heel Stone. No wonder some researchers think that early humans used Stonehenge as a calendar.

It's a 1.5 mile (2.4 km) walk from the visitor center to Stonehenge.

Visitors can only get up close to the stones during the annual summer solstice celebration, which lasts all night.

25

Weight in tons (22,680 kg) of the average large standing stone at Stonehenge.

- Stonehenge is a large circle of standing stones.
- Archaeologists believe that work began on Stonehenge about 5,000 years ago and lasted more than 1,000 years.
- Experts believe that Stonehenge may have been used as a holy site, observatory, healing place, or calendar.

Today, many of the stones remain standing in a circular pattern. No one knows why Stonehenge was built.

Some people believe it was a holy site. Others think it was a place to study the moon and stars. Another theory is that Stonehenge may have been a place of healing. Sick people would go there and hope to be cured. Archaeologists do know that Stonehenge served as a cemetery. They estimate about 200 people are buried at the site.

9

Nazca Lines Are Revealed from the Sky

The Nazca Lines in southern Peru are geoglyphs etched into the desert. A geoglyph is a design on the ground made by removing rocks and dirt. The lines form simple geometric shapes. Some are trapezoids. Others are rectangles or triangles. Some are straight while others are swirled. Some form animal shapes, such as a spider and a monkey.

Scientists believe that most of the lines were made by the Nazca people. They lived in the area from about 1 to 700 CE. The rocks that

It's believed the animal lines might have pointed to where there was water.

An observation tower allows visitors to have a bird's-eye view of the tree (*arbol*) and hands (*manos*).

THINK ABOUT IT

What methods do we use today to direct people to important places? Are different methods used in other countries? Do you think today's directions will still be used in the future?

cover the desert floor are a dark rust color. Removing the top layer reveals lighter-colored sand. The Nazca Lines have not changed much over the years. There is little wind or rain to erode them. The best place to view them is from high up, either from the air or on a nearby hilltop.

Some experts think the Nazca people may have used the lines to find their way. Maybe the lines pointed to places where they held water and crop rituals. Some of the animals in the Nazca Lines are associated with water. More study is needed to unravel the mystery of the Nazca Lines.

800

Number of straight lines in the Nazca Lines.

- Geoglyphs in southern Peru are known as the Nazca Lines.
- Scientists believe that the Nazca people, who lived from about 1 to 700 CE, made the lines.
- The Nazca people may have used the lines to find their way.

10

Terracotta Army Protects a Chinese Emperor

In 1974, a worker was digging a well outside Xi'an, China. Suddenly, he made one of the world's greatest archaeological discoveries. He unearthed a life-size clay soldier. When archaeologists arrived at the site, they found thousands of clay soldiers. An entire army of life-size terracotta soldiers and horses had been buried for more than 2,000 years.

The clay soldiers became known as the Terracotta Army. They were located near the unexcavated tomb of Qin Shi Huangdi. The first emperor of China, Qin ruled from 221 BCE to 210 BCE. Archaeologists believe that the clay soldiers were created to accompany him into the afterlife. Qin wanted to have the same military power there as he enjoyed during his lifetime. The army showed his glory and stood for the army he led to unite China.

More than 700,000 artisans and workers created the Terracotta Army

Each terracotta warrior has its own facial expression.

Pit 1 of the tomb is believed to hold up to 8,000 terracotta warriors.

and the emperor's tomb. They made the clay soldiers by hand. First, they built the soldiers' bodies. Then they added unique details. They added heads, hats, mustaches and ears. Each soldier was given his own facial expression. Each was positioned by rank. Patches of paint suggest that they once had brightly-colored clothing. Swords, arrow tips, and other weapons have been found in the excavations.

So far, three vaults holding parts of the Terracotta Army have been uncovered. The Terracotta Army is one of China's greatest attractions.

40

Estimated number of years it took to complete the Terracotta Army.

- The Terracotta Army was buried for more than 2,000 years.
- Archaeologists believe that the Chinese created the clay soldiers to accompany their emperor into the afterlife.
- Artisans added details to make each soldier unique.

11

Mysterious Moai Stand on Easter Island

On an island in the southeast Pacific Ocean, hundreds of statues stand in silence. The island is Rapa Nui, also known as Easter Island. The human-faced statues are called moai. The Rapa Nui people carved them from rough, hardened volcanic ash. They are huge and heavy, averaging 13 feet (4 m) tall and weighing 14 tons (12.7 metric t). The statues were placed on platforms called ahus.

Scientists believe that Rapa Nui made the moai between 1400 and 1600 CE. Many of the moai stand along the

Over time, the bodies of many moai statues became partially buried in sediment and rock.

An unfinished moai at a quarry on the island.

coast with their backs to the sea. Experts think they were meant to honor people within the Rapa Nui.

No one knows exactly why the Rapa Nui took on such a big challenge. Some experts suspect they carved the moai to honor their ancestors, chiefs, and other important people. The moai may have been a way for the Rapa Nui to communicate with their gods. Because the statues stand between Earth and the sky, they connect earthly chiefs with heavenly gods.

WEATHER DAMAGE

The moai of Easter Island are decaying. Their carvings are disappearing. The statues are being worn away by wind, rain, and sun. Weather effects have damaged the moai over many years. Conservation efforts will be needed to preserve these world treasures.

887

Total number of moai found on Easter Island.

- Mysterious statues called moai stand on Easter Island.
- Scientists believe that the Rapa Nui people created the moai between 1400 and 1600 CE.
- The moai are slowly being destroyed by the weather.

12

Petroglyphs Are Found at Legend Rock

Hot Springs County, Wyoming is the home of Legend Rock State Petroglyph Site. It is one of the most important petroglyph sites in the world. Petroglyphs are rock carvings. They are made by chipping away at rock with a stone chisel and a hammerstone. Removing the rock's surface reveals lighter-colored rock.

The Legend Rock site is a cliff about 1,312 feet (400 m) high and almost vertical. It holds more than 92 sandstone panels carved with petroglyphs. The prehistoric panels contain more than 300 images. Archaeologists believe the petroglyphs were carved over several thousand years. The earliest are about 11,000 years old. The most recent date from the mid-19th century. The oldest known images are an

The petroglyphs are sacred to the Shoshone Indians, shown here between 1908 and 1919.

Native Americans have been creating petroglyphs here for thousands of years.

antelope, a human figure, and a life-size hand.

For thousands of years, Legend Rock has been a sacred place for Native Americans who live in the region, such as the Shoshone people. Archaeologists are just beginning to decipher the carvings and what they mean. They hope the site will teach them more about the ancient peoples who lived in North America.

THINK ABOUT IT

If you were making a petroglyph, what images would you carve? What meaning do these images have for you? What would you hope other people would see in your petroglyphs?

1973

The year Legend Rock was named to the National Register of Historic Places.

- At Legend Rock in Wyoming, petroglyphs are carved into a vertical cliff.
- The oldest petroglyphs were made almost 11,000 years ago.
- For Native Americans, Legend Rock is a sacred site.

Where in the World?

The Legend Rock State Petroglyph Site in Wyoming features carvings made by Native American peoples who lived in the area.

Stonehenge in England is one of the world's most famous prehistoric monuments.

The Nazca Lines stretch in lines, shapes, and figures across the desert in southern Peru.

The Moai of Easter Island, carved thousands of years ago, stand along the coast of the volcanic island.

At Lascaux Cave in France, nearly 600 prehistoric cave paintings decorate the walls.

Gobekli Tepe in Turkey is believed to be the world's oldest temple.

The Masada complex holds well-preserved ruins from the ancient kingdom of Israel.

The Terracotta Army of life-size clay soldiers guards the tomb of China's first emperor, Qin Shi Huangdi.

The Pyramids of Giza were built as tombs for Egypt's pharaohs and hold many clues about ancient Egyptian life.

The Valley of the Kings in Egypt is one of the world's most famous groups of underground tombs.

Olduvai Gorge in Tanzania holds hundreds of fossils of early humans and stone tools.

Rising Star Cave in South Africa is the discovery site for *Homo naledi*, a new species of human.

Glossary

amphitheater
A theater, often with no roof, where seats are curved around in an oval or circle.

archaeologist
A person who studies past human life by examining things left by ancient peoples.

artifacts
Objects made by a human being, typically an item of cultural or historical interest.

besiege
To surround a place with armed forces in order to capture it or force the people to surrender.

excavation
The action of digging up or uncovering something.

fossils
The remains or impression of prehistoric organisms preserved in petrified form, or as a mold or cast in rock.

geoglyph
A drawing on the ground made by removing rocks and dirt to create an image.

gorge
A narrow valley between hills or mountains, typically with steep, rocky walls and a stream running through it.

megalith
A large stone that forms a prehistoric monument or part of one.

monolithic
Formed from a single large block of stone.

mummified
A body preserved after death by treating with chemicals and drying.

For More Information

Books

Hart, George. *Ancient Egypt.* New York: DK Publishing, 2014.

Jazynka, Kitson. *History's Mysteries: Curious Clues, Cold Cases, and Puzzles from the Past.* Washington, DC: National Geographic, 2017.

Yasuda, Anita. *Archaeology: Cool Women Who Dig.* White River Junction, VT: Nomad Press, 2017.

Index

About the Author

Carla Mooney is the author of many books for young readers. She loves investigating science and history and learning about new perspectives. A graduate of the University of Pennsylvania, Mooney lives in Pittsburgh with her husband and children.

READ MORE FROM 12-STORY LIBRARY

Every 12-Story Library Book is available in many formats. For more information, visit 12StoryLibrary.com